I'm Going To READ!™

These levels are meant only as guides;
you and your child can best choose a book that's right.

Level 1: Kindergarten–Grade 1 . . . Ages 4–6

- word bank to highlight new words
- consistent placement of text to promote readability
- easy words and phrases
- simple sentences build to make simple stories
- art and design help new readers decode text

Level 2: Grade 1 . . . Ages 6–7

- word bank to highlight new words
- rhyming texts introduced
- more difficult words, but vocabulary is still limited
- longer sentences and longer stories
- designed for easy readability

Level 3: Grade 2 . . . Ages 7–8

- richer vocabulary of up to 200 different words
- varied sentence structure
- high-interest stories with longer plots
- designed to promote independent reading

Level 4: Grades 3 and up . . . Ages 8 and up

- richer vocabulary of more than 300 different words
- short chapters, multiple stories, or poems
- more complex plots for the newly independent reader
- emphasis on reading for meaning

LEVEL 3

Library of Congress Cataloging-in-Publication Data Available

2 4 6 8 10 9 7 5 3 1

Published by Sterling Publishing Co., Inc.
387 Park Avenue South, New York, NY 10016
Text copyright © 2006 by Harriet Ziefert Inc.
Illustrations copyright © 2006 by Amanda Haley
Distributed in Canada by Sterling Publishing
c/o Canadian Manda Group, 165 Dufferin Street
Toronto, Ontario, Canada M6K 3H6
Distributed in Great Britain and Europe by Chris Lloyd at Orca Book
Services, Stanley House, Fleets Lane, Poole BH15 3AJ, England
Distributed in Australia by Capricorn Link (Australia) Pty. Ltd.
P.O. Box 704, Windsor, NSW 2756, Australia

I'm Going To Read is a trademark of Sterling Publishing Co., Inc.

Printed in China

Sterling ISBN 13: 978-1-4027-3081-8
Sterling ISBN 10: 1-4027-3081-0

For information about custom editions, special sales, premium and
corporate purchases, please contact Sterling Special Sales
Department at 800-805-5489 or specialsales@sterlingpub.com.

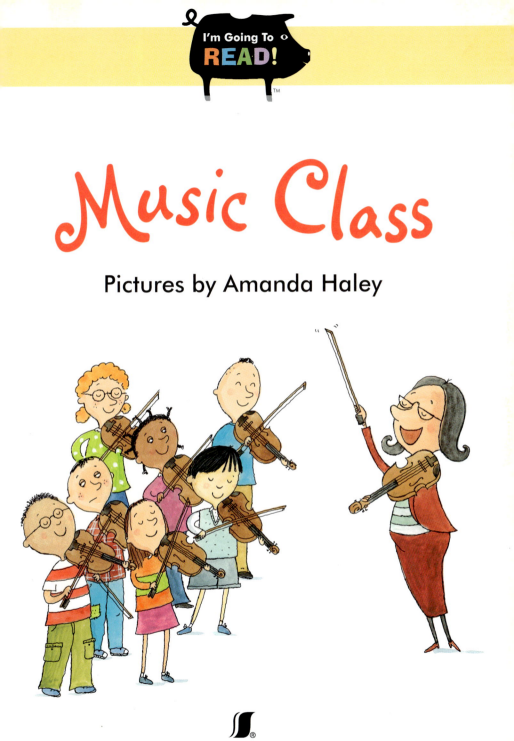

Music Class

Pictures by Amanda Haley

Sterling Publishing Co., Inc.
New York

Teacher says, "Come in. Come in.

It's time for your class in violin."

"Get your violins from their cases.

Hurry up and find your places!"

Each takes out violin and bow.

Do...re...mi...fa...so...la...ti...do!

Teacher plays a lovely tune.

All wish that they will learn it soon.

Teacher says:

"Before you can play the violin,
You must learn to hold it with your chin."

"Bows are held ever so lightly.
Never grip a bow too tightly."

Teacher signals ready to start.
Playing the violin is an art.

Music, music fills the air.

Pete and Susie really care.

Twinkle, twinkle, little star,

How I wonder what you are . . .

Up above the world so high,
Like a diamond in the sky . . .

Twinkle, twinkle, little star,
How I wonder what you are.

Johnny hears an awful ping.
It's the sound of a broken string!

Teacher says, "Okay, okay.
I will fix it so you can play."

Johnny's violin is really small,
But he dreams of Carnegie Hall.

Twinkle, twinkle, little star,
How I wonder what you are . . .

Up above the world so high,
Like a diamond in the sky . . .

Twinkle, twinkle, little star,
How I wonder what you are.

Teacher says, "All take a bow.

Bravo! Bravo!

Music class is over now."

Oh, how quickly time did fly.

Now it's time to say . . .

good-bye!